THE MASTER

was looking straight at him; down through the ages those grave, kind, sad, sweet eyes looked him through and through. The more John Stanley looked at the picture, the more power it seemed to have.

The Angel of His Presence

GRACE LIVINGSTON HILL

LIVING BOOKS
Tyndale House Publishers, Inc.
Wheaton, Illinois

Eighth printing, July 1988

Reprinted by permission of R. L. Munce Publishing Co.

Library of Congress Catalog Card Number 83-51594
ISBN 0-8423-0047-3, Living Books edition
Printed in the United States of America

*The angel
of his presence
saved them.
In his love
and in his pity
he redeemed them.*

ISAIAH 63:9

ONE

JOHN WENTWORTH STANLEY stood on the deck of an Atlantic liner looking off to sea and meditating. The line of smoke that floated away from his costly cigar followed the line of smoke from the steamer as if it were doing honest work to help get Mr. Stanley to New York. The sea in the distance was sparkling and monotonous and the horizon line empty and bright, but Mr. Stanley seemed to see before him the hazy outlines of New York as they would appear in about twenty-four hours more, if all went well. And of course all would go well. He had no doubt of that. Everything had always gone well for him.

Especially well had been these last two years of travel and study abroad. He reflected with satisfaction upon the knowledge and experience he had gained in his own special lines, upon the polish he had acquired, and he glanced over himself, metaphorically speaking, and found no fault in John Wentworth Stanley. He was not too Parisian in his deferential manner, he was not too English in his deliberation, neither was he, that worst of all traits in his eyes, too American in his bluntness. He had acquired something from each nation, and considered that the combined result was good. It is a comfortable feeling to be satisfied with one's self.

Nor had he been shut entirely out of the higher circles of foreign society. There were pleasant memories of delightful evenings within the noble walls of exclusive homes, of dinners and other enjoyable occasions with great personages where he had been an honored guest. When he thought of this, he raised his chest an inch higher and stood just a little straighter.

There was also a memory picture of one, perhaps more, but notably of one "ladye of high degree," who had not shown indifference to his various charms. It was pleasant to feel that one could if one would. In due time he would consider this question more carefully. In the near future this lady was to visit America. He had promised himself, and her, the pleasure of showing her a few of his own country's attractions. And— well, he might go abroad again after that on business.

His attention was not entirely distracted by his vision of the "ladye of high degree" from looking upon his old homeland and anticipating the scenes and the probable experiences that would be his in a few hours. Two years seemed a long time when he looked back upon it, though it had been brief in the passing. He would doubtless find changes, but there had been changes in him also. He was older; his tastes were— what should he say—developed? He would not take pleasure in the same way that he had taken it when he left, perhaps. He had learned that there were other things— things if not better, at least more cultured and less old-fashioned than his former diversions. Of course he did not despise his upbringing, nor his homeland, but he had other interests now as well, which would take much of his time. He had been from home long enough for the place he left to have closed behind him, and he would have no difficulty in staying "dropped out." He expected to spend much of his time in New York. Of course he would make his headquarters at home, where his father and mother were living, in a small city within a short distance of America's metropolis.

His man—he had picked up an excellent one while traveling through Scotland—had gone on ahead to unpack and put in place the various objects of art, and other treasures he had gathered on his travels. He had not as yet become so accustomed to the man that he could not do without him from day to day, and had found it convenient to send him home on the ship ahead of his own.

He wondered what his homecoming would be like. His father and mother would, of course, be glad to see him and give him their own welcome. But even with them he could not feel that he was coming home to a place where he was indispensable. They had other children, his brothers and sisters, married and living not far from home. Of course they would be glad to have him back, all of them, but they had been happy enough without him, knowing he was happy. But in town, while he had friends, there were none whom he eagerly looked forward to meeting. He had attended school there, of course, and in later years, after his return from college, had gone into the society of the place, the literary clubs and tennis clubs and, to a degree, into church work.

He had indeed been quite enthusiastic in church work at one time, had helped to start a mission Sunday school in a quarter where it was much needed, and had acted as superintendent up to the time when he went abroad. He smiled to himself as he thought of his "boyish enthusiasm," as he termed it, and turned his thoughts to his more intelligent manhood. Of course he would now have no time for such things. His work in the world was to be of a graver sort, to deal with science and art and literature. He was done with childish things.

He was interrupted just here by one of the passengers. "I beg your pardon. I have just discovered who you are and felt as if I would like to shake hands with you."

The speaker was a plain, elderly man with fine features and an earnest face. Mr. Stanley had noticed him casually several times and remarked to himself that that man would be quite fine looking if he would only pay a little more attention to his personal appearance. Not that he was not neatly dressed, nor that his handsome, wavy, iron-gray hair was not carefully brushed; but somehow John Wentworth Stanley had acquired during his stay abroad a nice discrimination in toilet matters, and liked to see a man with his trousers creased or not creased, as the height of the mode might demand, and classed him, involuntarily, accordingly.

But he turned in surprise as the stranger addressed him. What possible business could this man have with him, and what had he done that should make the man want to shake hands with him?

Mr. Stanley was courteous always, and he at once threw away the end of his finished cigar and accepted the proffered hand graciously, with just a tinge of his foreign-acquired nonchalance.

"My name is Manning. You don't know me. I came to live at Cliveden shortly after

" 'I have just discovered who you are and felt as if I
would like to shake hands with you.' "

you went abroad, but I assure you, I have heard much of you and your good work. I wonder I did not know you, Mr. Stanley, from your resemblance to your mother," the stranger added, looking into the young man's eyes with his own keen gray ones. He did not add that one thing which had kept him from recognizing his identity had been that he did not in the least resemble the Mr. Stanley he had been led to expect.

Mr. Manning owned to himself in the privacy of his stateroom afterward that he was just a little disappointed in the man, though he was handsome, and had a good face, but he did seem to be more of a man of the world than he had expected to find him. However, no trace of this was written in his kindly, interested face, as John Stanley endeavored to master the situation and discover what all this meant.

"Oh, I know all about your work in Cliveden, Mr. Stanley. I have been interested in the Forest Hill Mission from my first residence there, and what I did not learn for myself my little girl told me. She is a great worker, and as she has no mother, she makes me her confidant, so I hear all the stories of the trials and conflicts of her Sunday school class. Among other things I constantly hear of this one and that one who owe their Christian experience to the efforts of the founder of the mission and its first superintendent. Your crown will be rich in jewels. I shall never forget Joe Andrews' face when he told me the story of how you came to him Sunday after Sunday, and said, 'Joe, aren't you ready to be a Christian yet?' and how time after time he would shake his head. He says your face would grow so sad." The elder gentleman looked closely at the clean-shaven, cultured face before him to trace those lines which proved him to be the same man he was speaking of, and could not quite understand their absence, but went on, "And you would say, 'Joe, I shall not give you up. I am praying for you every day. Don't forget that.' And then when he finally could not hold out any longer and came to Christ, he says you were so glad, and he cannot forget how good it was of you to care for him and to stick to him that way. He said your face looked just as if the sun were shining on it the day he united with the church. That was a wonderful work you did there. It is marvelous how it has grown. Those boys of yours will someday repay the work you put upon them. Nearly all of the original members of your own class are now earnest Christians, and they cannot get done telling about what you were to them. My little girl writes me every mail more about it."

John Stanley suddenly felt like a person who is lifted out of his present life and set down in a former existence. All his tastes, his friends, his pursuits, his surroundings during the past two years had been utterly foreign to the work about which the stranger had been speaking. He had become so engrossed in his new life that he had actually forgotten the old. Not forgotten it in the sense that he was not aware of its facts, but rather forgotten his joy in it. And he stood astonished and bewildered, hardly knowing how to enter into the conversation, so utterly out of harmony with its spirit did he find himself. As the stranger told the story of Joe Andrews, there rushed over him the memory of it all: the boy's dogged face; his own interest awakened one day during his teaching of the lesson when he caught an answering gleam of interest in the boy's eye, and was seized with a desire to make Jesus Christ a real, living person to that boy's heart; his watching of the kindling spark in that sluggish soul, and how little by little it grew. Finally, one night the boy came to his home when there were guests present, and called for him, and he had gone out with him into the dewy night under the stars and sat down with him on the front piazza shaded by the vines, hoping and praying that this might be his opportunity to say the word that should lead the boy to Christ. Behold, he found that Joe had come to tell him, solemnly as though he were taking the oath of his life, that he now made the decision for Christ and hereafter would serve him, no matter what he wanted him to do. A strange thrill came with the memory of his own joy over that redeemed soul, and how it had lingered with him as he went back among his mother's guests, and how it would break out in a joyous smile now and then till one of the guests remarked, "John, you seem to be unusually happy tonight for some reason." How vividly it all came back now when the vein of memory was once opened. Incident after incident came to mind, and again he felt or remembered that

thrill of joy when a soul says, "You have
helped me to find Christ."

Mr. Manning was talking of his daughter. John had a dim idea that she was a
little girl, but he did not stop to question.
He was remembering. And there was a
strange mingling of feelings. His new char-
acter had so thoroughly impressed its importance upon him that he felt embarrassed
in the face of what he used to be. Strangely
enough the first thing that came to mind
was, What would the "ladye of high degree" think if she knew all this? She would
laugh. Ah! That would hurt worse than
anything she could do. He winced almost
visibly under her fancied merriment. It
was worse than if she had looked grave, or
sneered, or argued, or anything else. He
could not bear to be laughed at, especially
in his new role.

Somehow his old self and his new did not
seem to fit rightly together. But then the
new love of the world and his new tastes
came in with all the power of a new affec-
tion and asserted themselves, and he
straightened up haughtily and told himself
that of course he need not be ashamed of
his boyhood. He had not done anything but

Grace Livingston Hill

good. He should be proud of that, and especially so as he would probably not come in contact with such work and such people again. He had more important things to attend to.

Not that he said all this, or thought it in so many words; it passed through his mind like phantoms chasing one another. Outwardly he was the polished, courteous gentleman, listening attentively to what this father was saying about his daughter, though really he cared little about her. Did Mr. Stanley know that she had taken his former Sabbath school class and that there were many new members, among them some young men from the foundries? No, he did not. He searched in his memory and found a floating sentence from one of his mother's letters about a young woman who had consented to take his class till his return and who was doing good work. It had been written perhaps a year ago, and it had not concerned him much at the time as he was so engrossed in his study of the architecture of the south of France. He recalled it now just in time to tell the father how his mother had written him about the class, and so save his reputation as a Sunday

19

school teacher. It transpired that the daughter who had taken the class and the little girl the stranger so constantly referred to as writing him letters about things were one and the same. He wondered vaguely what kind of a little girl was able to teach a class of young men, but his mind was more concerned with something else now.

It appeared that the former mission where he had been superintendent had grown into a live Sunday school, and that they were looking for his homecoming with great joy and expectation. How could such a thing be other than disconcerting to the man he had become? He had no time to be bothered with his former life. He had his life work to attend to, which was not—and now he began to feel irritated—mission Sunday schools. That was all well enough for his boyhood, but now—and besides there was the "ladye of high degree."

Perhaps the man of experience saw the stiffening of the shoulders and the upper lip and divined the thoughts of the other. His heart sank for his daughter and her boys, and the mission, and their plans for his homecoming, and he made up his mind that secret or no secret, this man must be told a little of the joy of sacrifice that had been going on for him, for surely he could not have been the man that he had been, and not have enough of goodness left in his heart to respond to that story, no matter what he had become. And so he told him as much of the story his daughter had written him as he thought necessary, and John Wentworth Stanley thanked him and tried to show that he was properly appreciative of the honor that was to be shown him. He tried not to show his annoyance about it all to the stranger, and got away as soon as possible, after a few polite exchanges of farewells for the evening, and went to his stateroom. Arrived there, he seated himself on the side of his berth, his elbows on his knees, his chin in his hands, and sat scowling out of the porthole with anything but a cultured manner.

"Confound it all!" he muttered to himself. "I suppose it's got to be gone through with some way for mother's sake and after they've made so much fuss about it all. I can see it's all that girl's getting up; some silly girl that thinks she's going to become prominent by this sort of thing. Going to

give me a present! And I've got to go up
there and be bored to death by a speech
probably, and then get up and be made a
fool of while they present me with a pickle
dish or a pair of slippers or something of
the sort. It's awfully trying. And they
needn't think I'm going back to that kind of
thing, for I'm not. I'll move to New York
first. I wish I had stayed in France! I wish
I had never worked in Forest Hill Mission!"

Oh, John Stanley! Sorry you ever labored
and prayed for those immortal souls, and
wrought into your crown imperishable
jewels that shall shine for you through all
eternity!

TWO

THEY stood in the gallery of one of New York's most famous art stores; seven stalwart boys—young men, perhaps, you would call them—all with an attempt at "dress up," and with them Margaret Manning, slender and grave and sweet. They were chaperoned by Mrs. Ketchum, a charming little woman who knew a great deal about social laws and customs, and always spoke of things by their latest names, if possible, and who took the lead in most of the talk by virtue of her position in society and her supposed knowledge of art. There were also Mrs. Brown, a plain woman who felt deeply the responsibility of the occasion, and Mr. Talcut, a little man who was shrewd in business and who came along to see that they did not get cheated. These constituted the committee to select a present for the home-returning superintendent of the Forest Hill Mission Sunday school. It was a large committee and rather too heterogeneous to come to a quick decision, but its size had seemed necessary. Margaret Manning was on it, of course. That had been a settled thing from the beginning. There would not have been any such gift, probably, if Margaret had not suggested it and helped to raise the money till their fund went away up above their highest hopes.

The seven boys were in her Sunday school class, and no one of them could get the consent of himself to make so momentous a decision for the rest of the class without the other six to help. Not that these seven were her entire class by any means, but the class had elected to send seven from their own number, so seven had come. Strictly speaking, only one was on the committee, but he depended upon the advice of the other six to aid him.

"Now, Mr. Thorpe," said Mrs. Ketchum

in her easy, familiar manner, "we want something fine, you know. It's to hang in his 'den.' His mother has just been refitting his den, and we thought it would be quite appropriate for us to get him a fine picture for the wall."

They had already dispensed with the formalities. Mr. Thorpe knew the Stanley family slightly, and was therefore somewhat fitted to help in the selection of a picture that would suit the taste of one of its members. He had led them to the end of the large, well-lighted room, placed before them an easel, and motioned them to sit down.

The seven boys, however, were not accustomed to such things, and they remained standing, listening and looking with all their ears and eyes. Somehow, as Mrs. Ketchum stated matters, they did not feel quite as much to belong to this committee as before. What, for instance, could Mrs. Ketchum mean by Mr. Stanley's "den"? They had dim visions of Daniel and the lions, and the man who fell among thieves, but they had not time to reflect over this, for Mr. Thorpe was bringing forward pictures.

"As it's a Sunday school superintendent, perhaps something religious would be appropriate. You might look at these first, anyway," and he put before them a large etching whose wonder and beauty held them silent as they gazed. It was a new picture of the Lord's Supper by a great artist, and the influence of the picture was so great that for a few moments they looked and forgot their own affairs. The faces were so marvelously portrayed that they could but know each disciple, and felt that the hand which had drawn the Master's face must have been inspired.

"It is more expensive than you wanted to buy, but still it is a fine thing and worth the money. Perhaps, as it is for a church, I might make a reduction, that is, somewhat, if you like it better than anything else."

Mrs. Ketchum lowered her lorgnette with a dissatisfied expression, though her face and voice were duly appreciative. She really knew a fine thing when she saw it.

"It is wonderful, and you are very kind, Mr. Thorpe; but do you not think that perhaps it is a little, just a little, well—gloomy —that is, solemn—well—for a den, you know?" and she laughed uneasily.

Mr. Thorpe was accustomed to being all things to all men. With an easy manner he laughed understandingly.

"Yes? Well, I thought so myself, but then I didn't know how you would feel about it. It would seem hardly appropriate, now you think of it, for a room where men go to smoke and talk. Well, just all of you step around to this side of the room, please, and I'll show you another style of picture."

They followed obediently, Mrs. Ketchum murmuring something more about the inappropriateness of the picture for a den, and the seven boys making the best of their way among the easels and over Mrs. Ketchum's train. All but Margaret Manning. She lingered as if transfixed before the picture. Perhaps she had not even heard what Mrs. Ketchum had said. Two of the boys hoped so in whispers to one another.

"Say, Joe," he whispered in a low grumble, "I forgot all about Mr. Stanley's smoking. She——" with a nod toward the silent, preoccupied woman still standing in front of the picture, "she won't like that. Maybe he don't do it anymore. I don't reckon 'twould be hard fer him to quit."

Every one of those seven boys had given up the use of tobacco to please their teacher, Miss Manning.

Other pictures were forthcoming. There were landscapes and seascapes, flowers and animals, children and wood nymphs, dancing in extraordinary attitudes. The boys wondered that so many pictures could be made. They wondered and looked and grew weary with the unusual sight, and wished to go home and get rested, and did not in the least know which they liked. They were bewildered. Where was Miss Manning? She would tell them which to choose, for their part of the choice was a very important part to them, and in their own minds they were the principal part of the committee.

Miss Manning left the great picture by and by and came over to where the others sat, looking with them at picture after picture, hearing prices and painters discussed, and the merits of this and that work of art by Mrs. Ketchum and Mr. Talcut, whose sole idea of art was expressed in the price thereof, and who knew no more about the true worth of pictures than he knew about the moon. Then she left the others and

"She lingered as if transfixed before the picture."

wandered back to the quiet end of the room where stood that wonderful picture. There the boys one by one drifted back to her and sat or stood about her quietly, feeling the spell of the picture themselves, understanding in part, at least, her mood and why she did not feel like talking. They waited respectfully with uncovered heads, half bowed, looking, feeling instinctively the sacredness of the theme of the picture. Four of them were professed Christians, and the other three were just beginning to understand what a privilege it was to follow Christ.

Untaught and uncouth as they were, they took the faces for likenesses, and Christ's life and work on earth became at once to them a living thing that they could see and understand. They looked at John and longed to be like him, so near to the Master and to receive that look of love. They knew Peter and thought they recognized several other disciples, for the Sunday school lessons had become as vivid for them as mere words can paint the life of Christ. They seemed themselves to stand within the heavy arch of stone over that table, so long ago, and to be sitting at the

table—his disciples, some of them un-
worthy, but still there. They had been
helped to this by what Miss Manning had
said the first Sunday she took the class,
when the lesson had been of Jesus and of
some talks he had had with his disciples.
She had told them that as there were just
twelve of them in the class she could not
help sometimes thinking of them as if they
were the twelve disciples, especially as one
of them was named John and another
Andrew, and she wanted them to try to feel
that these lessons were for them; that
Jesus was sitting there in their class each
Sabbath speaking these words to them and
calling them to him.

The rest of the committee were coming
toward them, calling to Miss Manning in
merry, appealing voices. She looked up to
answer, and the boys who stood near her
saw that her eyes were full of tears. More
than one of them turned to hide and brush
away an answering tear that seemed to
come from somewhere in his throat and
choke him.

"Come, Margaret," called Mrs. Ketchum, "come and tell us which you choose.
We've narrowed it down to three, and are

pretty well decided which one of the three we like best."

Margaret Manning arose reluctantly and followed them, the boys looking on and wondering. She looked at each of the three. One was the aforementioned nymph's dance, another was a beautiful woman's head, and the third was a flock of children romping with a cart and a dog and some roses. Margaret turned from them disappointed, and looked back toward the other picture.

"I don't like any of them, Mrs. Ketchum, but the first one. Oh, I do think that is the one. Please come and look at it again."

"Why, my dear," fluttered Mrs. Ketchum, disturbed, "I thought we settled it that that picture was too, too—not quite appropriate for a den, you know."

But her words were lost, for the others had gone forward under the skylight to where the grand picture stood, and were once more under the spell of those wonderful eyes of the pictured Master.

"It is a real nice picture," spoke up Mrs. Brown. She was fond of Margaret Manning, though she did not know much about art. She had been elected from the women's

Bible class, and had been rather over-powered by Mrs. Ketchum, but she felt that now she ought to stand up for her friend Margaret. If *she* wanted that picture, that picture it should be.

"How much did you say you would give us that for, Mr. Thorpe?" said the sharp little voice of Mr. Talcut.

Mr. Thorpe courteously mentioned the figures.

"That's only ten dollars more'n we've got," spoke up the hoarse voice of one of the seven unexpectedly. It was Joe, who felt that he owed his salvation to the young superintendent's earnest efforts in his behalf.

"I say we'd better get it. Ten dollars ain't much. We boys can go that much. I'll go it myself somehow if the others don't."

"Well, really, ladies, I suppose it's a very good bargain," said Mr. Talcut, rubbing his hands and smiling.

"Then we'll take it," said Joe, nodding decidedly to Mr. Thorpe. "I'll go the other ten dollars, and the boys can help, if they like."

"But really Margaret, my dear," said Mrs. Ketchum quite distressed, "a *den*, don't you know, is not a place for——"

But the others were all saying it was just the picture, and she was not heard. Mr. Talcut was giving the address and orders about the sending. None of them seemed to realize that Mrs. Ketchum had not given her consent, and she, poor lady, had to gracefully accept the situation.

"Well, it's really a very fine thing, I suppose," she said at last, somewhat hesitatingly, and putting up her lorgnette to take a critical look. "I don't admire that style of architecture, and that tablecloth isn't put on very gracefully; it would have been more artistic draped a little. But it's really very fine, and quite new, you say, and of course the artist is irreproachable. I think Mr. Stanley will appreciate it."

But she sighed a little disappointedly, and wished she had been able to coax them to take the nymphs. She would take pains to let Mr. Stanley know that this had not been her choice. The idea of having to give in to those great boors of boys! But then it had all been Margaret Manning's fault. She was such a little fanatic. She might have known that it would not do to let her see a religious picture first.

THREE

IT was Margaret Manning's suggestion that it should be presented quietly. Some of the others were disappointed. Mrs. Ketchum was one of the most irate about it.

"The idea! After the school has raked and scraped together the money, that they should not have the pleasure of seeing it presented! It's a shame! Margaret Manning has some of the most backwoods' notions I ever heard of. It isn't doing things up right at all. There ought to be a speech from someone who knows how to say the right thing; my husband could have done it, and would if he'd been asked. But no, Margaret Manning says it must be hung on his wall, and so there it hangs, and none of us to get the benefit. I declare it is a shame! I wish I had refused to serve on that committee. I hate to have my name mixed up in it the way things have gone." So said Mrs. Ketchum as she sat back in her dim and fashionable parlor and sighed.

But the seven boys ruled things, and they ruled them in the way Miss Manning suggested. Moreover, Mrs. Brown and Mr. Talcut had gone over to the enemy completely since the purchase, the enemy being Miss Manning. Mr. Talcut rubbed his hands admiringly, and said Miss Manning was an exceedingly shrewd young woman, that she had an eye for business. That picture was the best bargain in that whole store.

But Margaret went on her way serenely, not knowing her power nor enjoying her triumph. Nevertheless, she was pleased in her heart with the picture, and she thought that her seven boys had been the true selectors of it. She wrote in her fine, even hand, that was like her in its lovely daintiness, the words the committee told her to write—which she had suggested—on a white card to accompany the picture. It read, "To our beloved superintendent, with a joyous welcome home, from the entire school of the Forest Hill Mission."

The Stanley home stood in fine, large grounds, with turf smooth as velvet and grand old forest trees all about. The house was large, old-fashioned, and ugly, but the rooms were magnificent in size, and filled with all the comforts money could buy. On one side, just off the large library and connected with the hall, had been built an addition, a beautiful modern room filled with nooks and corners and unexpected bay-windows, which afforded views in at least three directions because of the peculiar angles at which they were set. In one corner was a carved oak spiral staircase by which one could ascend to the airy sleeping room overhead if he did not choose to go through the hall and ascend the common stair. One side of the room and various other unexpected bits of wall were turned into bookcases sunk in the masonry and covered by glazed doors. The bay window seats were heavily upholstered in leather, and so were all the chairs and the luxurious couch. Nearly one entire end of the room was filled by the great fireplace, the tiling of which had been especially designed for it. In a niche built for it with a fine arrangement for light, both by day or night, stood a large desk. It was a model working room for a gentleman. And this addition had been built by the senior Mr. Stanley for his son when he should return to take up the practical work of architecture, for which he had been preparing himself for some years.

It was here that the great picture was brought and hung over the fireplace, where it could look down upon the entire room. It was hung just the day before John Wentworth Stanley's man arrived with his master's goods and chattels and began to unpack and dispose things according to his best judgment.

John Stanley's mother had come in to superintend the hanging of the picture and had looked at it a long time when she was left alone, and finally had knelt shyly beside the great new leather chair and offered a silent little prayer for the homecoming son. She was an undemonstrative woman, and this act seemed rather theatrical when she thought of it afterward. What if a servant had opened the door and seen her! Nevertheless she felt glad she had dedi-

cated the room, and she was glad that the
picture was what it was. With that Ketchum woman on the committee she had
feared what the result might be when the
scheme had been whispered to her. Some-
body must have fine taste. Perhaps it was
that dainty, lily-faced young girl who
seemed to be so interested in John's Sunday school class. Mrs. Stanley was busy in
her home world and did not go into church
work much. She was getting old and her
children and grandchildren were all about
her, absorbing her time and thought.

The man came in from the piazza that
surrounded the bay window and reached
around to the long French window at the
side, where he had been unpacking a box.
He placed a silver-mounted smoking set on
a small mahogany table. Then he stood back
to survey the effect. Presently he came in
with some fine cut glass, a small decanter
heavily mounted in silver and glasses to
match. He went out and came back with
their tray. Having dusted them off carefully and arranged them on the tray, he
placed it first on the handsome, broad mantel, and as before stood back to take a
survey. He knew the set was a choice

example of artistic work along this line. It had been presented to his master while he was visiting in the home of a nobleman, in token of his friendship and to commemorate something or other, the man did not exactly know what. But he did not like the effect on the mantel. He glanced uneasily up at the picture. In a dim way he felt the incongruity. He scowled at the picture and wondered why they put it there. It should have been hung in the hall or some out-of-the-way place. It was more suited for a church than anywhere else, he told himself. He placed the decanter tray on the little table at the other side of the fireplace from the smoking set, and stood back again. It looked well there. He raised his eyes defiantly to the picture, and met the full, strong, sweet gaze of the pictured eyes of the Master.

The man lowered his eyes and turned away, disturbed, he knew not why. He was not a man who cared about such things, neither was he one accustomed to reason. He went out to the piazza again to his unpacking, trying to think of something else. It wasn't his picture nor his decanter anyway, and he whistled a home tune and wondered why he had come to this country. He didn't seem to feel quite his usual pride this morning in the fact that he knew his business. When he finally unpacked the wicker-covered demijohn of real old Scotch whiskey that had accompanied the decanter, he carried it through the room and deposited it in the little corner cupboard behind the chimney, shut the door and locked it with a click, and went out again without so much as raising his eyes. All that day he avoided looking at that picture over the mantelpiece, and he grew quite happy in his work again and quite self-satisfied, and felt with a sort of superstitious fear that if he looked at it his happiness would depart.

There were other rare articles that he had to unpack and dispose of, and once he came to a large, handsome picture, a sporting scene in water colors by a celebrated artist. That now, would be the very thing to hang over the mantel in place of the picture already there. He even went so far as to suggest to Mrs. Stanley that he make the change, but she coldly told him to leave the picture where it was, as it was a gift, and showed him the envelope to place on the mantel directly under the picture, which contained the card from the donors.

So the man left the room at last, somewhat dissatisfied, but feeling that he had done the best he could. The night passed, the day came, and with it the new master of the new room.

"It's really a magnificent thing, mother," he said, as he stood in front of the great picture after having admired the room and shown his delight in all they had done for him. "I'm delighted to have it. I saw the original on the other side. And it was good taste of them to give it quietly in this way, too. But there is a sense in which this is quite embarrassing. They will expect so much, you know, and of course I haven't time for this sort of thing now."

"Well, I thought something ought to be done, my son," responded the mother, "so I sent out invitations for the whole school for a reception here next week. That is, I have them ready. They are not sent out, but are waiting your approval. Tuesday will be a free evening. What do you think?"

John Stanley scowled and sighed.

"Oh, I suppose that's the easiest way to

get out of it, now they've sent me this. It will be an awful bore, but then it'll be over. I shall scarcely know how to carry myself among them, I fear; I've been out of this line so long, and they fancy me so virtuous." He smiled and shrugged his handsome shoulders.

"But, John dear, you mustn't feel that way. They really think a great deal of you," said his mother, smiling indulgently upon him.

"Oh, it's all right; go ahead, mother. Make it something fine while you're about it. Give them quite a spread, you know. Some of them don't get many treats, I suppose," and he sank down in one of the luxurious chairs and looked about him with pleasure.

"This is nice, mother," he said; "so good of you and father to think of it. I can do great things here. The room is an inspiration in itself. It is a poem in architecture."

Then the mother left him awhile to his thoughts and he began to piece together his life, that portion he had left behind him across the water, and this new piece, a part of the old, that he had come to take up again. There hovered on the margin of his mind the image of the "ladye of high degree," and he looked about on his domain with satisfaction at thought of her. At least she would see that people in this country could do things as well as in hers.

Then by some strange line of thought he remembered his worriment of yesterday about that present, and how he had thought of her laugh if she should know of it. A slight feeling of pleasure passed over him; even in this she could find no fault. It was fine and costly and a work of genius. He need not be ashamed even if someone should say to her that the picture was presented to him by a mission class grateful for what he had done for it. He began to swell with a sense of importance at the thought. It was rather a nice thing, this present, after all. He changed his position that he might examine the picture more carefully at his leisure.

The fire that his mother had caused to be lighted to take off the chill of the summer evening and complete the welcome of the room, sent out a ruddy glow and threw into high relief the rich, dark gloss of the frame and the wonderful picture. It was as if the somber, stone-arched room opened directly

from his own, and he saw the living forms
of the Twelve gathered around that table
with the Master in the midst. But the
Master was looking straight at him—at
him, John Wentworth Stanley, self-satisfied gentleman of the world that he was—
looking at him and away from the other
disciples. Down through all the ages those
grave, kind, sad, sweet eyes looked him
through and through, and seemed to sift his
life, his every action, till things that he had
done now and yesterday, and last year,
that he had forgotten, and even when he
was a little boy, seemed to start out and
look him in the face behind the shadows
of those solid stones of that upper chamber.
The more he looked the more he wondered
at the power the picture seemed to have.
He looked away to prove it, and he knew
the eyes were following his.

The rosy glow of the firelight seemed to
be caught and crystallized in a thousand
sparkles on one side of the fire. He looked
in passing and knew what the sparkles
were, the fine crystal points of that cut
glass decanter. He had forgotten its existence until now, since the day he had had it
packed. He knew it was a beautiful thing in

its way, but he had not intended that it should be thus displayed. He hoped his mother had not seen it. He would look at it and then put it away, that is, pretty soon. Now his eyes were held by the eyes of his Master. Yes, his Master, for he had owned his name and called himself a Christian, and no matter what other things had come in to fill his mind, he had no wish to give up the "name to live." And yet he was conscious, strangely, abnormally conscious of that decanter. His Master seemed to be looking at it too, and to be inquiring of him how he came to have it in his possession. For the first time he was conscious, painfully so, that he had never given its donor any cause to think that such a gift would be less acceptable to him than something else. His Master had understood that too, he felt sure. He was annoyed that he could frame no excuse for himself, as he had so easily done when the gift first reached him. He had even been confident that he would be able to explain it to his mother so that she would be rather pleased with the gift than otherwise, strong temperance woman though he knew her to be. Now all his reasons had fled. The eyes of his Master, his kind, loving, sorrowing Master were upon him. He began to be irritated at the picture. He arose and seized the decanter hastily, to put it somewhere out of sight, just where he had not thought.

Now the officious Thomas, who knew his place and his work so well, had placed in the new, freshly washed decanter a small quantity of the rare old Scotch whiskey that had come with it. Thomas knew good whiskey when he saw—that is, tasted—it, and he was proud of a master to whom such a gift had been given. John Stanley did not expect to find anything in his decanter until he put it there himself, or gave orders to that effect. He was new to the ways of a "man" who so well understood his business. As he jerked the offending article toward him, some of this whiskey spilled out of the top that had perhaps not been firmly closed after Thomas had fully tested the whiskey. Its fumes so astonished its owner that, he knew not how, he dropped the decanter and it shivered into fragments at his feet on the dull red tiles of the hearth.

Annoyed beyond measure, and wondering why his hand had been so unsteady, he rang the bell for Thomas and ordered him to take away the fragments and wipe the whiskey from the hearth. Then he seated himself once more till it was done. And all the time those eyes, so sad and reproachful now, were looking through and through him.

"Thomas!" he spoke sharply, and the man came about face suddenly with the broom and dustpan in hand on which glittered the crystals of delicate cutting. "Where is the rest of that—that stuff?"

Thomas understood. He swung open the little door at the side of the chimney. "Right here at hand, sir! Shall I pour you out some, sir?" he said, as he lifted the demijohn.

John Stanley's entire face flushed with shame. His impulse was severely to rebuke the impertinence, nay the insult, of the servant to one who had always been known as a temperance man. But he reflected that the servant was a stranger to his ways, and that he himself had perhaps given the man reason to think that it would be acceptable by the very fact that he had these things among his personal effects. Then too, his eyes had caught the look of the Master as he raised them to answer, and he could not

"He dropped the decanter and it shivered into fragments at his feet."

speak that harsh word quite in that tone with Jesus looking at him.

He waited to clear his throat, and answered in a quieter tone, though still severely: "No; you may take it out and throw it away. I never use it."

"Yes, sir," answered Thomas impassively; but he marveled. Nevertheless he forgave his master, and took the demijohn to his own room. He was willing to be humble enough to have it thrown away on him. But as he passed the servant's piazza, the cook who sat resting from her day's labors there and planning for the morrow's menu, heard him mutter:

"As shure as I live, it's the picter. It's got some kind o' a spell."

FOUR

AFTER Thomas had left the room with the demijohn, his master seemed relieved. He began to walk up and down his room and hum an air from the German opera. He wanted to forget the unpleasant occurrence. After all, he was glad the hateful, beautiful thing was broken. It was no one's fault particularly, and now it was out of the way and would not need to be explained. He walked about, still humming and looking at his room, and still that picture seemed to follow and be a part of his consciousness wherever he went. It certainly was well hung, and gave the strong impression of being a part of the room itself. He looked at it critically from a new point of view, and as he faced it, once more he was in the upper chamber and seemed to hear his Master saying, "Yet a little while, and the world seeth me no more"; and he realized that he was in the presence of the scene of the end of his Master's mission. He walked back to the fireplace seeking for something to turn his thoughts away, and passing the table where stood his elegantly mounted smoking set, he decided to smoke. It was about the usual hour for his bedtime smoke, anyway. He selected a cigar from those Thomas had set out and lighted it with one of the matches in the silver match safe, and for an instant turned with a feeling of lazy, delicious luxury in the use of his new room and all its appliances. Unconsciously he seated himself again before the fire in the great leather chair, and began to puff the smoke into dreamy shapes and let his thoughts wander as he closed his eyes.

Suppose, ah, suppose that someone, say the "ladye of high degree," should be there, should belong there, and should come and stand behind his chair. He could see the graceful pose of her fine figure. She might reach over and touch his hair and laugh lightly. He tried to imagine it, but in spite of him the laugh rang out in his thoughts scornfully like a sharp, silver bell that belonged to someone else. He glanced over his shoulder at the imagined face, but it looked cold above the smoke. She did not mind smoke. He had seen her face behind a wreath of smoke several times. It seemed a natural setting. But the dream seemed an empty one. He raised his head and settled it back at a new angle. How rosy the light was as it played on the hearth and how glad he was to be at home again. That was enough for tonight. The "ladye of high degree" might stay in her home across the sea for this time. He was content.

Then he raised his eyes to the picture above without knowing it, and there he was smoking at the supper table of the Lord. At least so he felt it to be. He had always been scrupulously careful never to smoke in or about a church. He used to give long, earnest lectures on the subject to some of the boys of the mission who would smoke cigarettes and pipes on the steps of the church before service. He remembered them now with satisfaction, and he also remembered a murmured, jeering sound that had arisen from the corner where the very worst boys sat, which had been suppressed by his friends, but which had cut at the time, and which he had always wondered over a little. He had seen no inconsistency in speaking so to the boys in view of his own actions. But now, as he looked at that picture he felt as though he were smoking in church with the service going on. The smoke actually hid his Master's face. He took down his cigar and looked up with a feeling of apology, but this was involuntary. His irritation was rising again. The idea of a picture upsetting him so! He must be tired or his nerves unsettled. There was no more harm in smoking in front of that picture than before any other. "Confound that picture!" he said, as he rose and walked over to the bay window, "I'll have it hung somewhere else tomorrow. I won't have the thing around. No, it'll have to be left here till after that reception, I suppose; but after that it shall go. Such a consummate nuisance!"

He stood looking out of the open window with a scowl. He reflected that it was a strange thing for him to be so affected by a picture, a mere imagination of the brain. He would not let it be so. He would overcome it. Then he turned and tramped deliberately up and down that room, smoking away as hard as he could, and when he thought his equilibrium was restored, he raised his eyes to the picture as he passed, just casually as anyone might who had never thought of it before. His eyes fell and he went on, back and forth, looking every time at the picture, and every time the eyes of that central figure watched him with that same sad, loving look. At last he went to the window again and angrily threw up the screen, threw his half-smoked cigar far out into the shrubbery of the garden, saying as he did so, "Confound it all!"

It was the evening before the reception. It was growing toward nine o'clock, and John Stanley had retired to his wing to watch the fire and consider what a fool he was becoming. He had not smoked in that room since the first night of his return. He had not yielded to such weakness all at once nor with the consent of himself. He had thought at first that he really chose to walk in the garden or smoke on the side piazza, but as the days went by he began to see that he was avoiding his own new room. And it was all because of that picture. He glanced vengefully in the direction where it hung. He did not look at it willingly now if he could help it. His elegant smoking set was reposing in the chimney cupboard, locked there with a vicious click of the key by the hand of the young owner himself.

It was not only smoking, but other things that the picture affected. There for instance was the pack of cards he had placed upon the table in their unique case of dainty mosaic design. He had been obliged to put them elsewhere. They seemed out of place. Not that he felt ashamed of the cards. On the contrary he had expected to be quite proud of the accomplishment of playing well which he had acquired abroad, having never been particularly led in that direction by his surroundings before he had left home. Was this room becoming a church that he could not do as he pleased? Then there had been a sketch or two and a bit of statuary which he had brought in his trunk because they had been overlooked in the packing of the other things. That morning he brought them down to his room, but the large picture refused to have them there. There was no harm in the sketches, only they did not fit into the same wall with the great picture, there was no harmony in their themes. The statuary was associated with heathenism and wickedness, true, but it was beautiful and would have looked wonderfully well on the mantel against the rich, dark red of the dull tiles, but not under that picture. It was becoming a bondage, that picture, and after tomorrow night he would banish it to—where? Not his bedroom, for it would work its spell there as well.

Just here there came a tap on the windowsill, followed by a hoarse, half-shy whisper:

"Mr. Stanley, ken we come in?"

He looked up, startled. The voice had a familiar note in it, but he did not recognize the two tall, lank figures outside in the darkness, clad in cheap best clothes and with an air of mingled self-depreciation and self-respect.

"Who is it?" he asked sharply and suspiciously.

"It's me, Mr. Stanley; Joe Andrews. You ain't forgot me yet, I know. And this one's

my friend, Bert; you know him all right too.
May we come in here? We don't want to go
to the front door and make trouble with
the door bell and see folks; we thought
maybe you'd just let us come in where you
was. We hung around till we found your
room. We knowed the new part was yours,
'cause your father told the committee, you
know, when they went to tell about the
picture."

Light began to dawn on the young man.
Certainly he remembered Joe Andrews,
and had meant to hunt him up someday
and tell him he was glad to hear he was
doing well and living right, but he was in
no mood to see him tonight. Why could he
not have waited until tomorrow night when
the others were to come? Was not that
enough? But of course he wanted to get a
word of thanks all his own. It had been on
his tongue to tell Joe he was unusually busy
tonight, and would he come another time,
or wait till tomorrow, but the remembrance of the picture made that seem un-
gracious. He would let them in for a few
minutes. They probably wished to report
that they had seen the picture in the room
before the general view should be given, so

" 'Who is it?' he asked, sharply and suspiciously."

he unfastened the heavy French plate window and let the two in, turning up as he did so the lights in the room, so that the picture might be seen.

They came in, lank and awkward, as though their best clothes someway hurt them, and they did not know what to do with their feet and the chairs. They did not sit down at first, but stood awkwardly in single file, looking as if they wished they were out now they were in. Their eyes went immediately to the picture. It was the way of that picture to draw all eyes that entered the room, and John Stanley noted this with the same growing irritation he had felt all day. But over their faces there grew that softened look of wonder and awe and amazement, and, to John Stanley's surprise, of deep-seated, answering love to the love in the eyes of the picture. He looked at the picture himself now, and his fancy made it seem that the Master was looking at these two, well pleased. Could it be that he was better pleased with these two ignorant boys than with him, John Stanley, polished gentleman and cultured Christian that he trusted he was?

He looked at Joe again and was reminded of the softened look of deep purpose the night Joe had told him beneath the vines of his intention to serve Christ, and now standing in the presence of the boy again and remembering it all vividly, as he had not done before, there swept over him the thrill of delight again that a soul had been saved. His heart, long unused to such emotions, felt weak, and he sat down and motioned the boys to do the same. It would seem that the sight of the picture had braced up the two to whatever mission theirs had been, for their faces were set in steady purpose, though it was evident that this mission was embarrassing. They looked at one another helplessly as if each hoped the other would begin, and at last Joe plunged in.

"Mr. Stanley, you ben so good to us we thought 'twas only fair to you we should tell you. That is, we thought you'd like it, and anyway, maybe you wouldn't take it amiss."

John Stanley's heart was kind, and he had been deeply interested in this boy once. It all came back to him now, and he felt a strong desire to help him on, though he wondered what could be the nature of his errand.

Joe caught his breath and went on. "You see, she don't know about it. She's heard so much of you, and she never heard that, not even when they was talking about the den and all at the store, she was just lookin' at the picture and him," raising his eyes reverently to the picture on the wall, "and we never thought to tell her afore, and her so set against it. And we thought anyway afterward maybe you'd quit. Some do. We all did, but that was her doin'. But we thought you'd like to know, and if you had quit she needn't never be told at all, and if you hadn't, why we thought maybe 'twouldn't be nothin' for you to quit now, 'fore she ever knew about it."

The slow red was stealing up into the face of John Stanley. He was utterly at a loss to understand what this meant, and yet he felt that he was being arraigned. And in such a way! So humbly and by such almost adoring arraigners that he felt it would be foolish and wrong to give way to any feeling of irritation, or indignation, or even offended dignity on his part.

"I do not understand, Joe," he said at last, looking from one to another of the two boys who seemed too wretched to care to live longer. "Who is she? And what is it that she does not know, and that you want me to 'quit'? And why should it be anything to her, whoever she is, what I do?"

"Why it's her, Miss Manning—Margaret Manning—our teacher." Joe spoke the name slowly, as if he loved it and revered it. "And it's that we want you to—that is, we want her to—to like you, you know. And it's the—the—I can't most bear to say it, 'cause maybe you don't do it anymore," and Joe looked up with eyes like a beseeching dog.

"It's the smokin'," broke in Bert huskily, rising. "Come on, Joe, we've done what we 'greed to do; now 'tain't no more of our business. I say, come on!" and he bolted through the window shamefacedly.

Joe rose and going up to Mr. Stanley laid hold of his unwilling hand and choked out: "You won't take it hard of me, will you? You've done so much fer me, an' I kind of thought I ought to tell you, but now since I seen yer face I think maybe I had no business. Good-night," and with a face that looked as if he had been caught in the act of stealing, Joe followed his friend through the window and was lost in the deep shadows outside.

John Stanley stood still where the two had left him. If two robbers had suddenly come in upon him and quietly stolen his watch and diamond stud and ring and left him standing thus, he could not have looked more astonished. Where had been his usual ready anger that it did not rise and overpower these two impudent young puppies, ignorant as pigs, that they should presume to dictate to him, a Christian gentleman, what habits he should have? And all because some straitlaced old maid, or silly chit of a girl who loved power, did not like something. Where was his manhood that he had stood and let himself be insulted, be it ever so humbly, by boys who were not fit for him to wipe his feet upon? His kindling eyes lifted unexpectedly to the picture. The Master was watching him from his quiet table under the arches of stone. He stood a minute under the gaze and then he turned the lights all out and sat down in the dark. The fire was out too, and only the deep red glow behind the coals made a little lighting of the darkness. And there in the dark the boy Joe's face came back clearly and he felt sorry he had not spoken some word of comfort to the wretched fellow who felt so keenly the meaning of what he had done. There had been love for him in Joe's look and he could not be angry with him now he remembered that.

Bit by bit the winter of his work for Joe came back, little details that he did not suppose he ever should recall, but which had seemed filled with so much meaning then because he had been working for a soul's salvation and with the divine love for souls in his heart. What joy he had that winter! How sorry he had been to leave it all and go away. Now he came to think of it, he had never been so truly happy since. Oh, for that joy over again! Oh, to take pleasure in prayer as he had done in those days! What was this that was sweeping over him? Whence came this sudden dissatisfaction with himself? He tried to be angry with the two boys for their part in the matter, and to laugh at himself for being influenced by them, but still he could not put it away.

A stick in the fire fell apart and scattered

a shower of sparks about, blazing up into a brief glow. The room was illuminated just for an instant and the face of the Christ shone out clearly before the silent man sitting in front of the picture. Then the fire died out and the room was dark and only the sound of the settling coals broke the stillness. He seemed to be alone with Christ, face to face, with his heart open to his Lord. He could not shrink back now nor put in other thoughts. The time to face the change in himself had come and he was facing it alone with his God.

FIVE

IT was the next evening, and the Forest Hill Mission had assembled in full force. They were there, from little Mrs. Brown in her black percale, even to Mrs. Ketchum, who had pocketed her pride, and in a low-necked gown with a long train was making the most of her position on the committee. She arranged herself to "receive" with John Stanley and his mother, ignoring the fact that Mrs. Brown and "those seven hobbledehoy boys" were also on the committee. Occasionally she deplored the fact that Miss Manning had not come, that she might also stand in a place of honor, but in her heart she was glad that Miss Manning was not present to divide the honors with herself. It appeared that Mr. Stanley was delighted with the picture, had seen its original abroad, and knew its artist. Such being the case, Mrs. Ketchum was delighted to take all the honor of having selected the picture, and had it not been for those truthtelling, enlightening seven boys, John Stanley might never have known to this day Margaret Manning's part in it.

None of the central group saw Margaret Manning slip silently in past the servant at the door, as they stood laughing and chatting among themselves after having shaken hands perfunctorily with the awkward, embarrassed procession headed by Mr. Talcut and the young minister who had recently come to the place.

When Margaret came downstairs she paused a moment in the hall, but as she saw they were all talking, she went quietly on into the new wing that had been for the time deserted by the company, and placed herself in front of the picture. She had spoken to Mrs. Stanley, who had been called upstairs to the dressing room for a moment just as she came in, and so did not feel obliged to go and greet the group of receivers at once. Besides, she wanted to have another good look at the picture before she should go among the people, and so lose this opportunity of seeing it alone.

From the first view it had been a great delight to Margaret Manning. She had never before seen a picture of her Master that quite came up to her idea of what a human representation of his face should express. This one did. At least it satisfied her as well as she imagined any picture of him, fashioned from the fancy of a man's brain, could do. And she was glad to find herself alone with it that she might study it more closely and throw her own soul into the past of the scene before her.

She had stood looking and thinking for some minutes thus when she heard a quick step at the door, not a sound as of one who had been walking down the broad highly-polished floor of the hallway, but the quick movement of a foot after one has been standing. She looked up and saw John Stanley coming forward with an unmistakable look of interest and admiration on his face.

He had made an errand to his library for

a book to show to the minister in order to get a little alleviation from Mrs. Ketchum's persistent monopolization. He had promised to lend the book to the minister, but there had been no necessity for giving it to him that minute, nor even that evening. As he walked down the hall he saw a figure standing in his library, so absorbed in contemplating the picture that its owner did not turn nor seem to be aware of his coming. She was slender and graceful and young. He could see that from the distance, but as he came to the doorway and paused unconsciously to look at the vision she made, he saw that she was also beautiful. It was not the ordinary beauty of the ordinary fashionable girl with whom he was acquainted, but a clear, pure, high-minded beauty whose loveliness was not merely of the outward form and coloring, but an expression of beauty of spirit.

She was dressed in white with a knot of black velvet ribbon here and there. She stood behind his big leather chair, her hands clasped together against one cheek and her elbows resting on the wide leather back. There were golden lights in her brown hair. Her eyes were looking ear-

"She stood behind his big leather chair, her hands clasped together against one cheek."

nestly at the picture, her whole attitude reminded him of a famous picture he had seen in Paris. He could but pause and watch it before either of them became self-conscious.

There was in her intent look of devotion something akin to the look he had seen the night before in the face of the boy Joe. He recognized it at once, and a feeling half of envy shot through him. Would that such a look might belong to his own face. But the remembrance of Joe brought another thought. Instantly he knew that this was Margaret Manning. With the knowledge came also the consciousness that he stood staring at her and must do so no more. He moved then and took that quick step which startled her and made her look toward him. As he came forward, he seemed to remember how he had sat in that chair smoking a few nights before, and how the vision of the "ladye of high degree" had stood where this young girl now was standing, only he knew somehow at a glance the superiority of this living presence.

A flush at the remembrance of his visitors of the night before and their errand crossed his face, and he glanced instinctively toward the chimney cupboard to see if the door was safely locked.

"I beg your pardon," he said, coming forward. "I hope I do not disturb you. I came for a book. This must be Miss Manning, I think. How comes it that I have not had the pleasure of an introduction? They told me you had not come. Yes, I met your father on the steamer coming over. Is he present this evening?"

It was the easy, graceful tone and way he had, the same that had elicited the notice of the "ladye of high degree," only somehow now he had an instinctive feeling that it would take more than a tone and a manner to charm this young woman, and as she turned her clear eyes upon him and smiled, the feeling grew that she was worth charming.

He began to understand the admiration of those awkward boys and the feeling that had prompted their visit of the night before, and to consider himself honored since he had a part in their admiration.

Margaret Manning was prepared to receive him as a friend. Had she not heard great things of him? And she knew him at once. There was a fine photograph of him given by his mother at the request of the school—and unknown to himself—hanging in the main room of the Forest Hill Mission.

Their conversation turned almost immediately upon the picture. John Stanley told how he had seen the original and its artist abroad, and how proud he was to be the owner of this copy. The disagreeable experiences he had passed through on account of it seemed to have slipped from his mind for the time being.

She listened with interest, the fine, intelligent play of expression on her face which made it ever an inspiration to talk with her.

"How you will enjoy reading over the whole account of the Last Supper right where you can look at that face," she said wistfully, looking up at the picture. "It seems to me I can almost hear him saying, 'Peace I leave with you, my peace I give unto you.' "

He looked at her wonderingly, and saw the mark of that peace which passeth understanding upon her forehead, and again there appeared to him in startling contrast his vision of the "ladye of high degree," and he pondered it afterward in his heart.

" 'And this is life eternal, that they might know thee, the only true God, and Jesus Christ, whom thou hast sent.' He said that in the upper room," she mused. After a moment she added, "Was it then, too, that he said, 'For I have given you an example that ye should do as I have done to you'? I can't quite remember," and her eyes roved instinctively about the elegantly furnished room in apparent search for something.

He divined her wish at once, and courteously went in search of a Bible, but in his haste and confusion could not lay his hand upon one immediately. He murmured some apology about not having unpacked all his books yet, but felt ashamed as soon as the words were uttered, for he knew in his heart the young girl before him would have unpacked her Bible among the very first articles.

At last he found a small old-fashioned, fine-print Bible tucked in a corner of a bookcase. It had been given him when he was a child by some Sunday school teacher and forgotten long ago. He brought it now, and with her assistance found the place.

"How I should enjoy studying this with the picture," said the girl, as she waited for him to turn to the chapter.

"And why not?" he asked. "It would be a great pleasure to have you feel free to come and study this picture as often as you like. And if I might be permitted to be present and share in the study it would be doubly delightful."

It was with the small open Bible on the chairback between them that the file of awkward boys discovered them as they came down the hall, hoping to find an empty and unembarrassing room where they might take refuge. They paused as by common consent, and stood back in the shadow of the hall, as if the place were too sacred for them to more than approach its entrance. Their two earthly admirations were conversing together, the Bible between them, and the wonderful picture looking down upon them. They stole silent, worshipful glances into the room and were glad.

Then came Mrs. Ketchum with rustling, perfumed robes and scattered dismay into their midst and broke up the brief and pleasant *tête-à-tête* to her own satisfaction and the discomfiture of all concerned.

SIX

THEY were all gone at last, and the house was settling to quiet. John Stanley went to his room, shut his door, and sat down to think.

It had not been the unpleasant occasion to which he had looked forward. He had not even been bored. He was astonished to find himself regarding the evening not only with satisfaction, but also with an unusual degree of exhilaration. It did seem strange to him, now that he thought about it, but it was true.

New interests were stirring within him. Or were they old ones? He had gathered that group of boys about him with their teacher, after Mrs. Ketchum had broken up his quiet talk with Miss Manning, and had talked with them about the places he visited in the Holy Land, dwelling at some length upon the small details of what he had seen in Jerusalem, and the probable scene of events connected with the picture.

He had grown interested as he saw the interest of his audience. He realized that he must have talked well. Was it the intent gaze of those bright, keen-eyed boys, listening and glancing now and again toward the picture with new interest, as they heard of the city and its streets where this scene was laid, that gave him inspiration? Or had his inspiration come from that other rapt, sweet face, with earnest eyes fixed on the picture, and yet showing by an occasional glance at the speaker that she was listening and liked it?

Yes, it had been a happy evening, and over all too quickly. He would have liked to escort Miss Manning to her home, but her pony phaeton, driven by a faithful old servant, came for her, so he missed that pleasure.

He found himself planning ways in which he might often meet this charming young

woman. And strange to say, the mission
with its various services stood out pleas-
antly in his mind as a means to this end.
Had he forgotten his firm resolution of a
few days past, that he would have no more
to do with that mission in any capacity
whatever?

If this question occurred to him he
waived it without excuse. He was pledged
to attend the session of the school for the
next Sabbath anyway, to give in more elab-
orate form the talk about the picture and
the scenes in Jerusalem of which he had
spoken to the boys. It had been Miss Manning's work, this promise, of course. She
had said how grand it would be to have him
to tell the whole school what he had told
her class, and had immediately interviewed
the present superintendent, who had been
only too delighted to accept the suggestion.

And now he sat by his fire, and with
somewhat different feelings from those he
had experienced a few evenings before,
thought over his old life and his new.
Strangely enough the "ladye of high degree" came no longer to his thoughts, but
instead there stood in shadow behind the
leather chair a slender, girlish figure with

an earnest face and eyes, and by and by he gave himself up to contemplating that, and he wondered no longer that the boys had given up many things to please her. He would not find it so very hard to do the same.

How earnest she had been! What a world of new meaning seemed to be invested in the sacred scene of that picture after she had been talking about it. He had followed up her desire to read the account with it in view, and begged her most eagerly to come and read it and let him be a humble listener, offering also in a wistful tone, which showed plainly that he hoped she would accept the former, to let her have the picture at her home for a time.

It would be very pleasant to read anything, even the Bible, with this interesting young person and study the workings of her mind. He could see that she was unusual. He must carefully study the subject so as not to be behind her in Bible lore, for it was likely she knew all about it, and he did not wish to be ashamed before her. He reached over to the table where he had laid the little fine-print Bible they had been consulting earlier in the evening. It had been so long since he had made a regular business of reading his Bible that he scarcely knew where to turn to find the right passages again, but after fluttering the leaves a few minutes he again came to the place and read: "Now when the even was come, he sat down with the twelve. And as they did eat, he said, Verily I say unto you, that one of you shall betray me."

The young man stopped reading, looking up at the picture involuntarily, and then dropped his eyes to the fire. What was it that brought that verse home to himself? Had he in any sense betrayed his Lord? Was it only the natural inquiry of the truthful soul on hearing those words from the Master and on looking into his eyes to say sorrowfully, "Lord, is it I?" or was there some reason for it in his own life that made him sit there, hour after hour, while the bright coals faded, and the ashes dropped away and lay still and white upon the hearth?

Thomas, the man, looked silently in once or twice, and marveled to find his master reading what seemed to be a Bible, and muttered, "That pictur," to himself as he went back to his vigil. At last he ventured to open the door and say in a respectful tone, "Did you call me, sir?" which roused the master somewhat to the time of night, and moved him to tell his man to go to bed and he would put out the lights.

The days that followed were filled with things quite different from what John Stanley had planned on his return voyage. He made a good start in his business, and settled into regular working hours, it is true; but in his times of leisure he quite forgot that he had intended to have nothing to do with the mission people. He spent three evenings in helping to cover Sunday school library books and paste labels into singing books. Prosaic work and much beneath him he would have considered it a short time ago, but he came home each time from it with an exhilaration of mind such as he had never experienced from any of the whist parties he had attended. It is true there were some young men and young women also pasting labels, whose society was uninteresting, but he looked upon even those with leniency. Were they not all animated by one common object, the good work for the mission? And there was also present and pasting with the others, with deft fingers and quiet grace, that one young girl around whom all the others seemed to gather and center as naturally as flowers turn to the sun. She seemed to be an inspiration to all the others.

John Stanley had not yet confessed that she was an inspiration to himself. He only admitted that her society was helpful and enjoyable, and he really longed to have her come and read those chapters over with him. Just how to manage this had been a puzzle. Whenever he spoke of it the young lady thanked him demurely, and said she would like to come and look at the picture sometime; but he had a feeling that she would not come soon, and would be sure he was not at home then before she ventured. This was right, of course. It was not the thing, even in America, for a young woman to call upon a young man even to read the Bible with him. He must overcome this obstacle. Having reached this conclusion he called in his mother to assist.

"By the way, mother," he said the next evening at dinner, "I met a very agreeable gentleman on the voyage over, a Mr. Manning. He is the father of the Miss Manning who was here the other evening, I believe. Do you know them? I wish you would have them to dinner some night. I would like to show him some courtesy."

The mother smiled and assented. It was easy for her to do nice little social kindnesses. And so it was arranged.

After dinner it was an easy thing for John Stanley to slip away to the library with Margaret Manning, where they two sat down together before the picture, this time with a large, fine leather edition of the Bible to read from.

That was an evening which to John Stanley was memorable through the rest of his life. He had carefully studied the chapters himself, and thought he had searched out from the best commentators all the bright new thoughts concerning the events that the imagination and wisdom of man had set down in books, but he found that his companion had studied on her knees, and that while she was not lacking either book knowledge or appreciation of what he had to say, she yet was able to open to him a deeper spiritual insight. When she was gone, and he sat alone in his room once more, he felt that it had been glorified by her presence. He lingered long before that picture with searchings of heart that meant much for his future life, and before he left the room he knelt and consecrated himself as never before.

In those days there were evening meetings in the mission and he went. There was no question in his mind about going; he went gladly, and felt honored when Mr. Manning was unable to escort his daughter and he was allowed to take his place. There was a nutting excursion for the school, and he and Miss Manning took care of the little ones together. When it was over he reflected that he had never enjoyed a nutting party more, not even when he was a care-free boy.

It came about gradually that he gave up smoking. Not that he had at any given time sat down and deliberately decided to do so, at least not until he found that he had almost done so. There was always some meeting or engagement at which he hoped to meet Miss Manning, and instinctively he shrank from having her know that he smoked, mindful of what his evening visitors had told him. At first he fell into the habit of smoking in the early morning as he walked in the garden, but once while thus engaged he saw the young woman coming down the street, and he threw away his cigar and disappeared behind the shrubbery, annoyed at himself that he was doing something of which he seemed to be ashamed. He wanted to walk to the fence and speak to her as she passed by, but he was sure the odor of smoke would cling to him. Little by little he left off smoking lest she would detect the odor about him. Once they had a brief conversation on the subject, she taking it for granted that he agreed with her, and someone came to interrupt them ere he had decided whether to speak out plainly and tell her he was one whom she was condemning by her words. His face flushed over it that night as he sat before his fire. She had been telling him what one of the boys had said when she had asked him why he thought he could not be a Christian: "Well, I can't give up smokin', and we know he never would 'a' smoked." That had seemed a conclusive argument to the boy.

Was it true that he was sure his Master never would have done it? Then ought he, a professed follower of Christ? He tried to say that Miss Manning had peculiar views

"He threw away his cigar and disappeared behind
the shrubbery."

on this subject and that those boys were unduly influenced by her; and he recalled how many good followers of Christ were addicted to the habit. Nevertheless, he felt sure that no one of them would advise a young man to begin to smoke and he also felt sure about what Jesus Christ would do.

It had been a long time since he had tried himself and his daily conduct with that sentence, "What would Jesus do?" He did not realize that he was again falling into the way of it. If he had, it might have made him too satisfied with himself.

There came to be many nights when he sat up late looking into the fire and comparing his life with the life of the Man whose pictured eyes looked down so constantly into his own. It was like having a shadow of Christ's presence with him constantly. At first it had annoyed him and hung over him like a pall, that feeling of the unseen Presence which was symbolized by the skillful hand of the artist. Then it had grown awesome, and held him from many deeds and words, nay even thoughts, until now it was growing sweet and dear, a presence of help, the eyes of a friend looking down upon him in all his daily actions, and unconsciously he was beginning to wonder whenever a course of conduct was presented to his mind whether it would seem right to Christ.

At last the happy winter was slipping away rapidly. He had scarcely stopped to realize how fast, until one night when letters had come in on the evening mail, one from England brought vividly to his mind some of his thoughts and resolves and feelings during that return voyage in the fall. He smiled to himself as he leaned back in the great leather chair and half-closed his eyes. How he had resolved to devote himself to art and literature and leave religion and philanthropy to itself! And he had devoted himself to literature, in a way. Had not he and Miss Manning and several others of the mission spent the greater part of the winter in an effort to put good pictures and books into the homes of the people of the mission, and also to interest these people in the pictures and books? He had delivered several popular lectures, illustrated by the best pictures, and had assisted at readings from our best authors. But would his broad and cultured friends from the foreign shore, who had so high an opinion of his ability, consider that a strict devotion of himself to art and literature? And as for the despised mission and its various functions, it had become the center of his life interest. He glanced up at the picture on his wall. Had it not been the cause of all this change in actions, his plans, his very feelings? Nay, had not its central figure, the Man of Sorrows, become his friend, his guide, his Savior in a very real and near sense?

And so he remembered the first night he had looked upon that picture and its strange effect upon him. He remembered some of his own thoughts minutely, his vision of that "ladye of high degree" with whose future his own seemed likely to be joined. How strange it seemed to him now that he could have ever dreamed of such a thing! Her supercilious smile seemed even now to make him shrink. The prospect of her trip to America in the spring or early summer was not the pleasant thing he had then thought it. Indeed, it annoyed him to remember how much would be expected of him as guide and host. It would take his time from things—and people—more correctly speaking, one person who had grown very dear. He might as well confess it to himself now as at any other time. Margaret Manning had become to him the one woman in all the earth whose love he cared to win. And looking on his heart as it now was, and thinking of himself as when he first returned from abroad, he realized that he was not nearly so sure of her saying, "Yes" to his request that she would give her life into his keeping, as he had been that the "ladye of high degree" would assent to that request.

Why was it? Ah! Of this one he was not worthy, so pure and true and beautiful a woman was she. While the other—was it possible that he had been willing to marry a woman about whom he felt as he did toward this other haughty woman of wealth and position? To what depths had he almost descended! He shuddered involuntarily at the thought.

By and by he arose and put out the light preparatory to going upstairs for the night, humming a line of an old song:

"The laird may marry his ladye, his ladye
     of high degree—
But I will marry my true love,"

and then his face broke into a sweet smile and he added aloud and heartily, "if I can" —and hummed the closing words, "For true of heart am I," as he went out into the hall, a look of determination growing on his face and the vision of Margaret Manning enshrined in his heart.

SEVEN

THE visit of the "ladye of high degree" to America was delayed by wind and tide and circumstance until the late fall, and in the meantime the people of America had not stood still for her coming.

Among other things that had been done, there had been put up and fully equipped a sort of clubhouse belonging to the Forest Hill Mission. It does not take long to carry out such schemes when there are two earnest persons with determination and ability to work like John Stanley and Margaret Manning.

The money for the scheme had come in rapidly and from unexpected sources. Margaret declared that every dollar was an answer to prayer.

The house itself was perfectly adapted for the carrying out of their plans of work. There were reading rooms and parlors where comfort and a certain degree of refinement prevailed. There was a gymnasium in which the privileges and days were divided equally between men and women, and where thorough instruction was given. There were rooms in which various classes were carried on evenings for those who had no chance otherwise, and there were even a few rooms for young men or young women, homeless and forlorn, where they could get good board for a time, and the whole was presided over by a motherly, gray-haired woman and her husband, whose hearts were in the work, and whose good common sense made them admirably fitted for such a position.

But amid all these plans and preparations for better work John Stanley had found opportunity to speak to Margaret Manning the words which had won her consent to make his home bright by her presence and his heart glad with her love.

Their wedding cards had traveled across

the ocean, passing midway the steamer that carried a letter from the "ladye of high degree," saying that she was about to embark on her trip to America and rather demanding John Stanley's time and attention during her stay near his home. She had been used to this in the days when he was near her home, and he had been only too glad to be summoned then.

Her letter waited for him several days while he was away on a short business trip, and it came about that he opened it but three days before his wedding day. He smiled as he read her orders. He was to meet her at the steamer on the fifteenth. Ah! that was the day when he hoped to be a hundred miles away from New York, speeding blissfully along with Margaret by his side. He drew a sigh of relief as he reached for pen and paper and wrote her a brief note explaining that he was sorry not to be able to show her the courtesies he had promised, but that he would be away on his wedding trip at the time. He afterward added an invitation from his mother, and closed the note and forgot all about the matter.

And so it was that the "ladye of high degree" instead of being met with all the devotion she had expected—and which she had intended to exact to its utmost—found only a brief note with a paltry invitation to his wedding reception. She bit her lips in vexation and spent a disagreeable day in a New York hotel, making all those who had to do with her miserable. Then she hunted up the names of other acquaintances in America, noted the date of that reception, and made up her mind to make her haughty best of it; at least, when she returned home there was the laird and the earl and the poor duke, if worst came to worst.

The Stanley home was alight from one end to the other, and flowers and vines did their best to keep up the idea of the departing summer indoors that night when John Stanley brought home his lovely bride.

It was a strange gathering and a large one. There were present of New York's best society the truest and best of men and women, whose costumes and faces showed that their purses and their culture were equally deep. And there were many people, poor and plain, in their best clothes, it is true, but so different from the others that one scarcely knew which costume was more out of place, that of the rich or of the poor.

It had been John Stanley's idea, and Margaret had joined in it heartily, this mingling of the different classes to congratulate them in their new life.

"They will all have to come together in heaven, mother," John had said in answer to Mrs. Stanley's mild protest at inviting Mrs. Cornelius Van Rensselaer together with Joe Andrews and the mill girls from the mission. "That is, if they all get there, and in my opinion Joe Andrews stands as good a chance as Mrs. Van Rensselaer. What is the difference? It will only be a little in their dress. I think all of our friends are too sensible to mind that. Let them wear what they please, and for once let us show them that people can mingle and be friends without caring for the quality of cotton or silk in which each one is wrapped."

The mother smiled and lifted her eyebrows a little. She could imagine the difference between those mill girls and the New York ladies, and she knew her son could not, but her position was established in the world, and she was coming to the age when these little material things do not so much matter. She was willing that her son should do as he wished. She only said in a lingering protest, "But their grammar, John. You forget how they murder the king's English."

"Never mind, mother," he said, "I shouldn't wonder if we should all have to learn a little heavenly grammar when we get there before we can talk fittingly with the angels."

And so their friends were all invited, and none belonging to the Forest Mission were omitted. Mrs. Ketchum, it is true, was scandalized. She knew how to dress, and she did not like to be classed among the "rabble," as she confided to a few of her friends. "However, one never knew what Margaret Manning would do, and of course this was just another of her performances. If John Stanley wasn't sorry before very long that he married that woman of the clouds, she would miss her guess."

She took it upon herself to explain in an undertone to all the guests, whom she considered worthy of the toilet she had prepared, that these "other people," as she denominated the Forest Hill Mission,

pointing to them with her point lace fan
with a dainty sweeping gesture, were
protégés of the bride and groom, and were
invited that they might have the pleasure
of a glimpse into the well-dressed world,
a pleasure probably that none of them had
ever had before.

The "ladye of high degree" was there,
oh, yes! Her curiosity led her, and her
own pique. She wanted to see what kind of
a wife John Stanley had married, and she
wanted to see if her power over him was
really at an end.

The rich elegance of her wonderful gown,
ablaze with diamonds and adorned with
lace of fabulous price, brushed aside the
dainty white of the bride's and threatened
to swallow it up out of sight in its own
glistening folds.

But the bride, in her filmy white robes,
seemed in no wise disturbed, neither did
her fair face suffer by contrast with the
proud, handsome one. The "ladye of high
degree," standing in the shadow studying
the sweet bride's face, was forced to admit
that there was a superior something in this
other woman that she did not understand.
She turned to John Stanley, her former

admirer, and found his eyes resting in undisguised admiration on the lovely face of
his wife, and her eyes turned again to the
wife and saw her kiss the wrinkled face of
an elderly Scotch woman with beautiful,
tender brown eyes and soft waving hair.
The neat, worn brown cashmere dress that
the woman wore was ornamented only by a
soft ruffle about the neck. The hair was
partly covered by a plain brown bonnet
with an attempt at gala attire in a bit of
white lace in front, and the wrinkled, worn
hands were guiltless of any gloves, but one
of those bare hands was held lovingly between the bride's white gloves, and the
other rested familiarly about the soft white
of the bride's waist. There was a beautiful
look of love and trust and appreciation in
both faces, and instinctively this stranger
was forced to ask the other onlooker, "Who
is she?"

"One of God's saints on earth," came
John Stanley's voice in answer. He had
been watching the scene and had forgotten
for the moment to whom he was talking.
Not that he would have disliked to speak
so to the "ladye of high degree" now, for he

was much changed, but he would not have thought she would understand.

"She is just a dear woman in the church whom my wife loves very much. She is a natural poet soul, and you may be sure she has been saying something to her which would be worth writing in a book, and which she will always remember."

And then the "ladye of high degree" turned and looked at her old acquaintance in undisguised astonishment. John Stanley must have noticed this and been embarrassed a moment, but Mrs. Ketchum came by just then to be introduced, and she proved to be the kindred spirit for whom this stranger had been searching. From her was gained much information, some of which astonished her beyond belief. She made one or two more attempts to rally her power over John Stanley later in the evening, but she too had fallen under the spell of the lovely woman whose eyes her husband's followed wherever she went, and she finally gave it up.

The final surprise came to the stranger guest late in the evening, as she was making her way through John Stanley's study to the cloak room. She had been told by the voluble Mrs. Ketchum that this room was Mr. Stanley's "den." She had also noticed during the evening at different times that people stopped opposite the picture that hung on the wall over the mantel. She had not before been in a position to see what this picture was for the crowd, but she had supposed it some masterpiece that Mr. Stanley had brought home from his travels. Her curiosity, or her interest, or both, led her to pause now alone, and to look up.

As others were held under its spell, so was this woman for a moment. The beauty and expression of the work of art caught her fancy, and the face of the Master held her gaze, while her soul recognized and understood the subject. In great astonishment she glanced around the room once more and back. Could it be that John Stanley kept a picture like this in his den? It was not like the John Stanley she had known.

And then a soft little white-gloved hand rested on her shoulder, and a sweet, earnest voice said: "Isn't it wonderful? I'm so glad to be where I can look at it every day as much as I wish."

Turning she saw the bride standing by her side. She scarcely knew how to answer, and before she could do so she noticed that another had entered the room, and she knew instinctively that Mr. Stanley had come.

"That is one of my treasures. Are you admiring it?" he said in the strong voice that seemed so unlike his old one, and the guest murmured something about the picture, and, looking about uneasily, excused herself and slipped away.

They stood a moment before the picture together, the husband and wife. They were tired with the evening's talk, and a sight of this refreshed them both and gave the promise of future joy.

The "ladye of high degree," passing through that hall, having purposely come by another route from the cloak room rather than through the study, saw them standing also, and understood—that she did not understand—and went out into the night with a lonely longing for something, she knew not what.

As the two stood together the husband said: "Do you know, dear, that picture has made the turning point in my life. Ever since it came in here I have felt that his presence was with me wherever I went. And I have you to thank for it all. And through it I have gained you, this richest, sweetest blessing of my life. Do you know, I found a verse in my Bible today that it seems to me fits me and that picture. It is this: 'The angel of his presence saved them. In his love and in his pity he redeemed them.' "

"The 'ladye of high degree'... saw them standing also."

Other Living Books Best-sellers

THE ANGEL OF HIS PRESENCE by Grace Livingston Hill. This book captures the romance of John Wentworth Stanley and a beautiful young woman whose influence causes John to reevaluate his well-laid plans for the future. 07-0047 $2.95.

ANSWERS by Josh McDowell and Don Stewart. In a question-and-answer format, the authors tackle sixty-five of the most-asked questions about the Bible, God, Jesus Christ, miracles, other religions, and creation. 07-0021 $3.95.

THE BEST CHRISTMAS PAGEANT EVER by Barbara Robinson. A delightfully wild and funny story about what happens to a Christmas program when the "Horrible Herdman" brothers and sisters are miscast in the roles of the biblical Christmas story characters. 07-0137 $2.50.

BUILDING YOUR SELF-IMAGE by Josh McDowell. Here are practical answers to help you overcome your fears, anxieties, and lack of self-confidence. Learn how God's higher image of who you are can take root in your heart and mind. 07-1395 $3.95.

THE CHILD WITHIN by Mari Hanes. The author shares insights she gained from God's Word during her own pregnancy. She identifies areas of stress, offers concrete data about the birth process, and points to God's sure promises that he will "gently lead those that are with young." 07-0219 $2.95.

COME BEFORE WINTER AND SHARE MY HOPE by Charles R. Swindoll. A collection of brief vignettes offering hope and the assurance that adversity and despair are temporary setbacks we can overcome! 07-0477 $5.95.

DARE TO DISCIPLINE by James Dobson. A straightforward, plainly written discussion about building and maintaining parent/child relationships based upon love, respect, authority, and ultimate loyalty to God. 07-0522 $3.50.

DAVID AND BATHSHEBA by Roberta Kells Dorr. This novel combines solid biblical and historical research with suspenseful storytelling about men and women locked in the eternal struggle for power, governed by appetites they wrestle to control. 07-0618 $4.95.

FOR MEN ONLY edited by J. Allan Petersen. This book deals with topics of concern to every man: the business world, marriage, fathering, spiritual goals, and problems of living as a Christian in a secular world. 07-0892 $3.95.

FOR WOMEN ONLY by Evelyn and J. Allan Petersen. Balanced, entertaining, diversified treatment of all the aspects of womanhood. 07-0897 $4.95.

400 WAYS TO SAY I LOVE YOU by Alice Chapin. Perhaps the flame of love has almost died in your marriage. Maybe you have a good marriage that just needs a little "spark." Here is a book especially for the woman who wants to rekindle the flame of romance in her marriage; who wants creative, practical, useful ideas to show the man in her life that she cares. 07-0919 $2.95.

Other Living Books Best-sellers

GIVERS, TAKERS, AND OTHER KINDS OF LOVERS by Josh McDowell and Paul Lewis. This book bypasses vague generalities about love and sex and gets right to the basic questions: Whatever happened to sexual freedom? What's true love like? Do men respond differently than women? If you're looking for straight answers about God's plan for love and sexuality, this book was written for you. 07-1031 $2.95.

HINDS' FEET ON HIGH PLACES by Hannah Hurnard. A classic allegory of a journey toward faith that has sold more than a million copies! 07-1429 $3.95.

HOW TO BE HAPPY THOUGH MARRIED by Tim LaHaye. One of America's most successful marriage counselors gives practical, proven advice for marital happiness. 07-1499 $3.50.

JOHN, SON OF THUNDER by Ellen Gunderson Traylor. In this saga of adventure, romance, and discovery, travel with John—the disciple whom Jesus loved—down desert paths, through the courts of the Holy City, to the foot of the cross. Journey with him from his luxury as a privileged son of Israel to the bitter hardship of his exile on Patmos. 07-1903 $4.95.

LIFE IS TREMENDOUS! by Charlie "Tremendous" Jones. Believing that enthusiasm makes the difference, Jones shows how anyone can be happy, involved, relevant, productive, healthy, and secure in the midst of a high-pressure, commercialized society. 07-2184 $2.95.

LOOKING FOR LOVE IN ALL THE WRONG PLACES by Joe White. Using wisdom gained from many talks with young people, White steers teens in the right direction to find love and fulfillment in a personal relationship with God. 07-3825 $3.95.

LORD, COULD YOU HURRY A LITTLE? by Ruth Harms Calkin. These prayer-poems from the heart of a godly woman trace the inner workings of the heart, following the rhythms of the day and the seasons of the year with expectation and love. 07-3816 $2.95.

LORD, I KEEP RUNNING BACK TO YOU by Ruth Harms Calkin. In prayer-poems tinged with wonder, joy, humanness, and questioning, the author speaks for all of us who are groping and learning together what it means to be God's child. 07-3819 $3.50.

MORE THAN A CARPENTER by Josh McDowell. A hard-hitting book for people who are skeptical about Jesus' deity, his resurrection, and his claims on their lives. 07-4552 $2.95.

MOUNTAINS OF SPICES by Hannah Hurnard. Here is an allegory comparing the nine spices mentioned in the Song of Solomon to the nine fruits of the Spirit. A story of the glory of surrender by the author of *HINDS' FEET ON HIGH PLACES*. 07-4611 $3.95.

NOW IS YOUR TIME TO WIN by Dave Dean. In this true-life story, Dean shares how he locked into seven principles that enabled him to bounce back from failure to success. Read about successful men and women—from sports and entertainment celebrities to the ordinary people next door—and discover how you too can bounce back from failure to success! 07-4727 $2.95.

Other Living Books Best-sellers

THE POSITIVE POWER OF JESUS CHRIST by Norman Vincent Peale. All his life the author has been leading men and women to Jesus Christ. In this book he tells of his boyhood encounters with Jesus and of his spiritual growth as he attended seminary and began his world-renowned ministry. 07-4914 $4.50.

REASONS by Josh McDowell and Don Stewart. In a convenient question-and-answer format, the authors address many of the commonly asked questions about the Bible and evolution. 07-5287 $3.95.

ROCK by Bob Larson. A well-researched and penetrating look at today's rock music and rock performers, their lyrics, and their life-styles. 07-5686 $3.50.

THE STORY FROM THE BOOK. The full sweep of *The Book's* content in abridged, chronological form, giving the reader the "big picture" of the Bible. 07-6677 $4.95.

SUCCESS: THE GLENN BLAND METHOD by Glenn Bland. The author shows how to set goals and make plans that really work. His ingredients of success include spiritual, financial, educational, and recreational balances. 07-6689 $3.50.

TELL ME AGAIN, LORD, I FORGET by Ruth Harms Calkin. You will easily identify with the author in this collection of prayer-poems about the challenges, peaks, and quiet moments of each day. 07-6990 $3.50.

THROUGH GATES OF SPLENDOR by Elisabeth Elliot. This unforgettable story of five men who braved the Auca Indians has become one of the most famous missionary books of all times. 07-7151 $3.95.

WAY BACK IN THE HILLS by James C. Hefley. The story of Hefley's colorful childhood in the Ozarks makes reflective reading for those who like a nostalgic journey into the past. 07-7821 $4.50.

WHAT WIVES WISH THEIR HUSBANDS KNEW ABOUT WOMEN by James Dobson. The best-selling author of *DARE TO DISCIPLINE* and *THE STRONG-WILLED CHILD* brings us this vital book that speaks to the unique emotional needs and aspirations of today's woman. An immensely practical, interesting guide. 07-7896 $3.50.

The books listed are available at your bookstore. If unavailable, send check with order to cover retail price plus $1.00 per book for postage and handling to:

Tyndale DMS
Box 80
Wheaton, Illinois 60189

Prices and availability subject to change without notice. Allow 4–6 weeks for delivery.